This book is dedicated to the many small communities across Wisconsin that make it such a special place. From my Grandma Wenzel up in St. Germain, to the Carey family down in Jefferson, to the memory of my Grandpa Grimm in Wild Rose, to my father's roots in East Troy, Wisconsin is built on those small communities and the Badger fans therein.

For my Mom and Dad: You are the best and I will forever be grateful for all that you have done for me.

Finally, for the city of Madison and the University of Wisconsin-Madison, which shaped my values and character in more ways than are imaginable: I have such fond memories of my college years, and this is my way of saying "thank you." On Wisconsin and Go Bucky! – CLN

ISBN 10: 0-9841196-1-2
ISBN 13: 978-0-9841196-1-5

Copyright © 2009 by University Pride Publishing

Book design by Robert Rath.

For more information, contact University Pride Publishing, 6699 MacArthur Drive, Missoula, MT 59808, or visit our website at www.universitypridepublishing.com

The University of Wisconsin-Madison is the sole owner of all trademark rights in Bucky Badger, the Badgers, the Motion W and other designations as may be used herein. These marks are used by permission of the University of Wisconsin-Madison.

Cataloging-in-Publication Data is on file at the Library of Congress.

Created, illustrated, produced and designed in the United States.
Printed in Korea.

First printing, July 2009

The Big Bucky Badger Mystery

WRITTEN BY
Chris Newbold

ILLUSTRATED BY
Robert Rath

UNIVERSITY PRIDE PUBLISHING

GAME TIME!

"Saturday is my big day," thought Bucky.

2

"I can hear it now – the siren of the Bucky wagon,
the thunder of the band, the roar of the crowd!"

Bucky's fur tingled with excitement.

Saturday was the first Badger football game of the fall!

He could hardly wait to see the sea
of cardinal red and white and the
excited faces of little Badger fans!

"**I** must get ready and pack my game bag. The players are counting on me," Bucky said as he got ready.

"Let's see. What do I need to bring with me to the game?"

"Extra sweater – check!"

"Dancing shoes – check!"

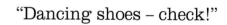

"The 'W' flag – check!"

"Football – uh oh!"

"Where's the football?"

5

Bucky had always been the badger in charge of the game day football.

The players trusted him to keep watch over the ball until it was time to play.

Bucky had taken extra-special care of the football all summer, making sure it was properly inflated and stored safely in his cool, dark den.

"Oh where, oh where
could that football be?"
worried Bucky.

"It's not in my den! It's a mystery!"

"I must retrace my steps," Bucky
reasoned. "Certainly I can find it
if I just search hard enough!
Now, where was I yesterday?
I'll start by looking there first,"
he planned.

Thinking back, Bucky remembered that he started his morning with a sail on the waters of Lake Mendota.

"That's it! Maybe I left it at Memorial Union!" he exclaimed.

Bucky Says **DID YOU KNOW?**

Lake Mendota has been referred to as the most studied lake in North America, with the UW-Madison limnology department (which studies freshwater bodies) on its southern bank. The lake is 9,842 acres in size and has a maximum depth of 84 feet.

Bucky began searching the Terrace.

Splish, splash, splish, splash. Bucky heard
the rippling of the waves behind him.

"Whew! Now where, oh where could that football be?"

Bucky looked under the tables and around
the chairs. There was no sign of
the football at the Terrace.

10

"Oh dear," said Bucky, "I must move quickly to find the ball in time for Saturday's game!"

"Where did I go next? After I finished sailing, I visited the Dane County Farmer's Market to pick up some berries."

"That's it! Maybe I left it near the Capitol!"

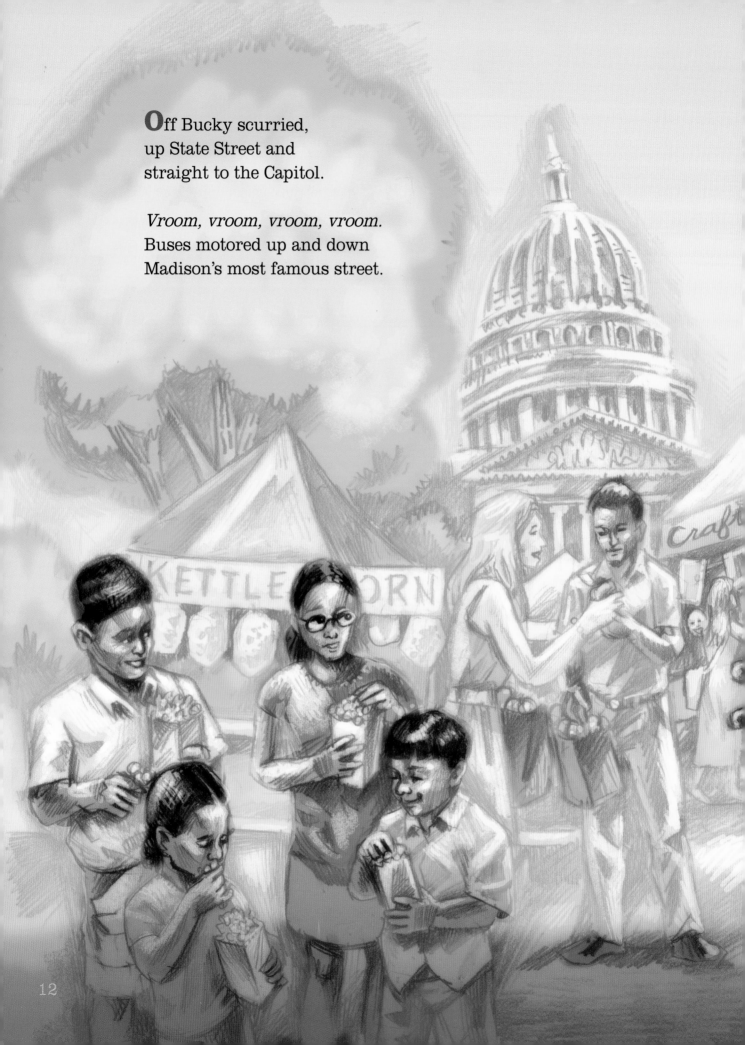

Off Bucky scurried,
up State Street and
straight to the Capitol.

Vroom, vroom, vroom, vroom.
Buses motored up and down
Madison's most famous street.

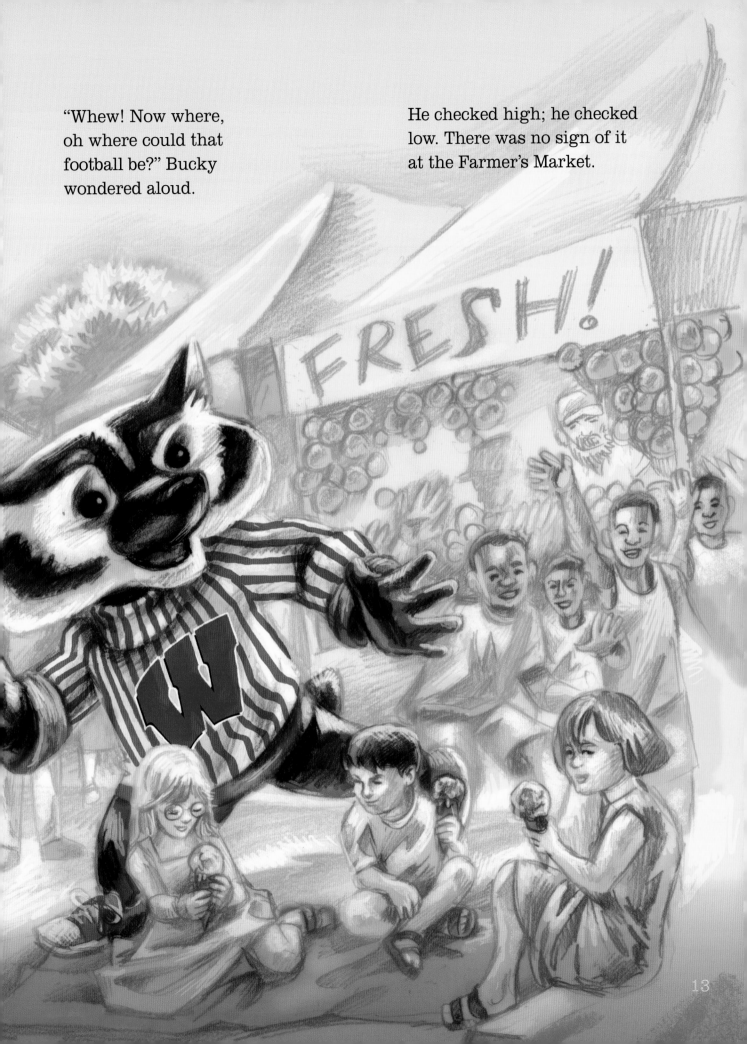

"Whew! Now where, oh where could that football be?" Bucky wondered aloud.

He checked high; he checked low. There was no sign of it at the Farmer's Market.

13

Still retracing his
previous steps,
Bucky concentrated,
"Where did
I go next?"

Bucky Says **DID YOU KNOW?**

The Wisconsin State Capitol is 284 feet,
5 inches tall from the ground floor to the
top of the statue on the dome, making it
only 3 feet shorter than the nation's Capitol in
Washington D.C. The Capitol was constructed of 43
types of stone from six countries and eight states.

"Aha! I remember! All that
hustling around downtown
made me hungry, and I met
up with my friends at the
zoo to eat lunch."

"That's it! Maybe I left it
at the Henry Vilas Zoo!"

Bucky continued his
search with his friends.

Eeeck, eeeck, eeeck, eeeck!
The monkeys squealed as
Bucky hurried by.

"Whew! Now where, oh where could that
football be?" pondered Bucky as he peered into
the bushes and poked through the branches.
There was no sign of it at the Zoo.

Bucky Says

DID YOU KNOW?

The Henry Vilas Zoo is one of only a few free admission zoos in the country accredited by the Association of Zoos and Aquariums. The Zoo receives over 500,000 visitors annually and celebrates its 100th anniversary in 2011.

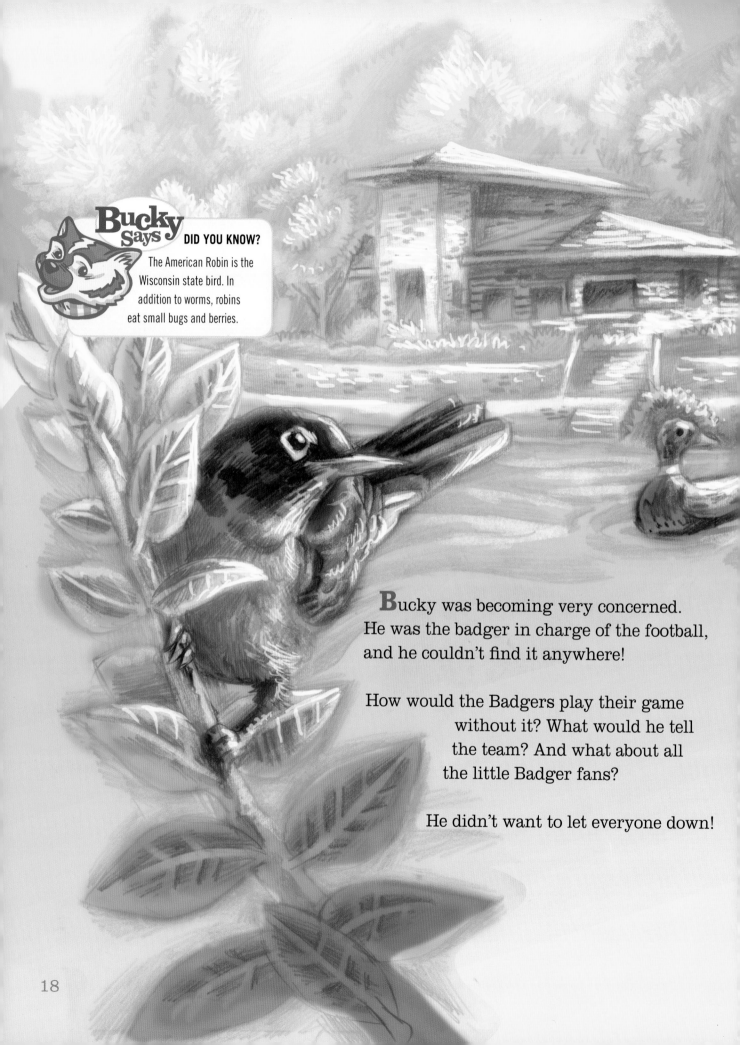

Bucky was becoming very concerned. He was the badger in charge of the football, and he couldn't find it anywhere!

How would the Badgers play their game without it? What would he tell the team? And what about all the little Badger fans?

He didn't want to let everyone down!

Bucky took a seat on the banks of Lake Wingra
to think hard about where he could have left the football.

Imagining the day before, Bucky recalled, "After I ate my lunch at the Zoo, I craved a little dessert. What better treat than a pint of Badger Blast ice cream at Babcock Hall? That's got to be it!"

"Maybe I left it on campus." Bucky raced past the dairy barn in his search for the ball.

Moo, moo, moo, moo. Several cows bellowed from the barn.

"Whew! Now where, oh where could that football be?" After ordering yet another ice cream, Bucky peered over the counters and under the coolers.

There was no sign of it at Babcock Hall.

DID YOU KNOW?
Gourmet ice cream has been created and sold on the University of Wisconsin campus for over 90 years and is frequently voted "Best in Madison" by *Madison Magazine*.

Time was running out!

Bucky pictured the
disappointed faces of all
the fans and wondered
what he should do.

22

"Maybe I could tell them the ball popped while I was practicing my push-ups," mused Bucky.

"Or maybe they'd believe me if I said I gave it away to a deserving little Badger fan," he schemed.

"I know! I can tell them a gopher stole the ball!"

After a few minutes of thinking up all of the ways he could explain the missing football . . .

Bucky realized what he had to do. He must tell the players what really happened.

23

Sadly, Bucky shuffled toward Camp Randall Stadium.

24

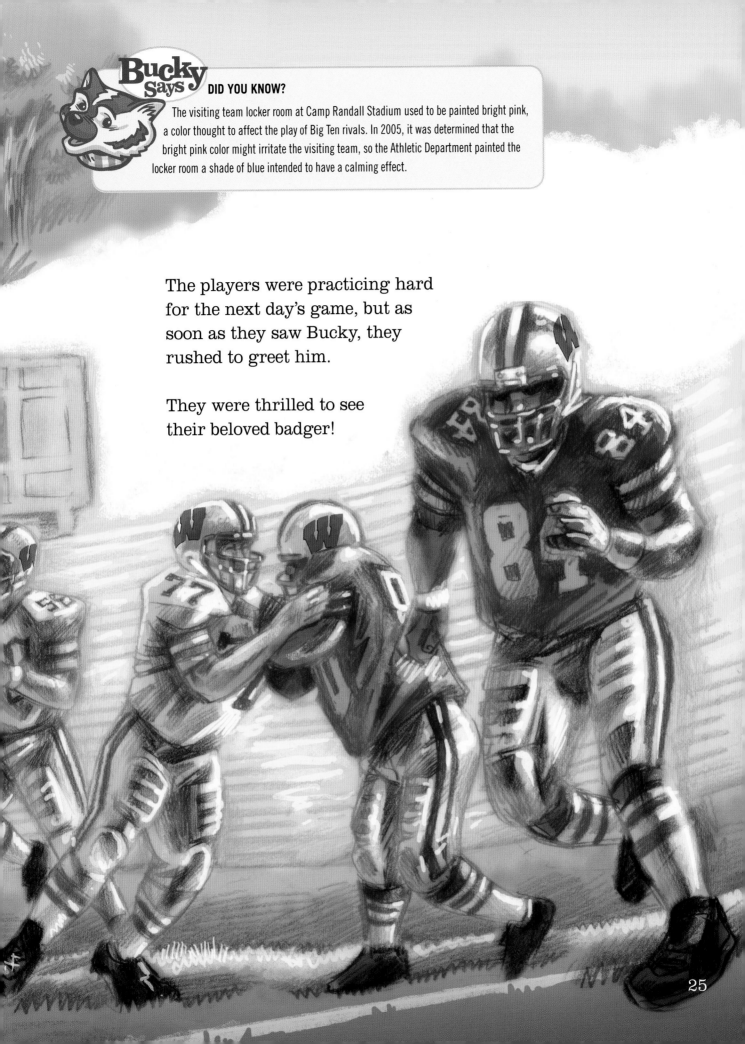

The players were practicing hard for the next day's game, but as soon as they saw Bucky, they rushed to greet him.

They were thrilled to see their beloved badger!

Bucky reluctantly shared the bad news. "Fellow Badgers, I must report to you that somehow, somewhere, I lost the game day football you entrusted to me. I am very sorry and hope I can make it up to you."

26

"Hey, Bucky," yelled the quarterback.
"Is this what you're looking for?"

Sailing across the football field
came the game day ball!

28

"I borrowed it yesterday for our
practice. I must have forgotten
to tell you," he said sheepishly.

Bucky leaped into the air! Hooray!
The mystery was solved.

He hadn't lost the football after all.

He was now ready to cheer on his
Badgers at Saturday's game!

Bucky Says

DID YOU KNOW?
Camp Randall Stadium can
hold over 80,000 screaming
Badger fans, so on game day
the football stadium becomes
the equivalent of the fifth-largest city
in Wisconsin.

The thrill of jumping around, the tradition
of singing "Varsity," the pride of the Fifth
Quarter – he could feel it now . . .

Sing along to The **University** of **Wisconsin** fight song!

On Wisconsin, On Wisconsin,
Plunge right through that line.

Run the ball clear down the field,
A touchdown sure this time. (U-Rah-Rah)

On Wisconsin, On Wisconsin,
Fight on for her fame.

Fight, fellows, fight, fight, fight,
We'll win this game.

On Wisconsin, On Wisconsin,
Stand up Badgers sing.

"Forward" is our driving spirit,
Loyal voices ring.

On Wisconsin, On Wisconsin,
Raise her glowing flame.

Stand, fellows, let us now
Salute her name.

We Want to Hear From You!

If your child, grandchild, niece, nephew, brother, sister or little Badger is a huge fan of *The Big Bucky Badger Mystery*, let us know. Please visit our website at **www.universitypridepublishing.com** and share your story. Select stories posted will receive a handwritten note from the author and a special sketch from the illustrator to your special Badger fan, as well as limited edition bookmarks and coloring sheets inspired by the book. On Wisconsin!